Harry
on Holiday

Chris Powling and Scoular Anderson

Collins

Best Friends · *Jessy and the Bridesmaid's Dress* · *Jessy Runs Away* · **Rachel Anderson**
Changing Charlie · *Clogpots in Space* · **Scoular Anderson**
Ernest the Heroic Lion-tamer · *Ivana the Inventor* · **Damon Burnard**
Weedy Me · **Sally Christie**
Almost Goodbye Guzzler · *Two Hoots* · **Helen Cresswell**
Magic Mash · *Nina's Machines* · **Peter Firmin**
Clever Trevor · *The Mystery of Lydia Dustbin's Diamonds* · *Nora Bone* ·
Nora Bone and the Tooth Fairy · **Brough Girling**
Sharon and Darren · **Nigel Gray**
Thing-in-a-Box · *Thing-on-two-legs* · **Diana Hendry**
Desperate for a Dog · *More Dog Trouble* · **Rose Impey**
Georgie and the Computer Bugs · *Georgie and the Dragon* ·
Georgie and the Planet Raider · **Julia Jarman**
Cowardy Cowardy Cutlass · *Free With Every Pack* · *Mo and the Mummy Case* ·
The Fizziness Business · **Robin Kingsland**
And Pigs Might Fly! · *Albertine, Goose Queen* · *Jigger's Day Off* ·
Martians at Mudpuddle Farm · *Mossop's Last Chance* ·
Mum's the Word · **Michael Morpurgo**
Granny Grimm's Gruesome Glasses · **Jenny Nimmo**
Grubble Trouble · **Hilda Offen**
Hiccup Harry · *Harry on Holiday* · *Harry's Party* · *Harry the Superhero* ·
Harry with Spots On · **Chris Powling**
Grandad's Concrete Garden · **Shoo Rayner**
Rattle and Hum – Robot Detectives · *Rattle and Hum in Double Trouble* · **Frank Rodgers**
The Father Christmas Trap · **Margaret Stonborough**
Our Toilet's Haunted · **John Talbot**
Pesters of the West · **Lisa Taylor**
Jacko · *Lost Property* · *Messages* · **Pat Thomson**
A Hiccup on the High Seas · **Karen Wallace**
Monty, the Dog who Wears Glasses · *Monty Bites Back* · *Monty Ahoy!* ·
Monty Must be Magic! · *Monty up to his Neck in Trouble* ·
Monty's Ups and Downs · **Colin West**
Bing Bang Boogie, it's a Boy Scout · *Ging Gang Goolie, it's an Alien* · *Stone the Crows, it's a*
Vacuum-cleaner · **Bob Wilson**

First published by A & C Black (Publishers) Ltd 1997
Published by Collins in 1998

10 9 8 7 6 5 4 3 2

Collins is an imprint of HarperCollins Publishers Ltd,
77/85 Fulham Palace Road, London W6 8JB

ISBN 0–00–675–350–7

Printed in Great Britain by
Clays Ltd, St Ives plc

My dad had never been so friendly.
He'd mended my bike,

helped me tidy
my room

and even come to
the park for a game
of football.

What's more, he'd been giggly the whole time – more like a big brother than a dad.

SO I WAS CONVINCED SOMETHING WAS WRONG.

That evening, while we were watching television, I found out what it was.

6

Mum looked cross.

'But you've had all day to do it –
you've been fiddling around with
his bike and his toys and his
football for ages.'

See what I mean about knowing
something was wrong?

So Dad explained about the money we'd spent on our new house and on my baby sister and on Christmas and on his extra fares to work.

I realised at once where it was leading.

NO HOLIDAY THIS YEAR.

Sometimes I really hate my mum.

To make things even worse, that evening's *Dream Holidays* turned out to be the best show ever. Debbie Dream, the presenter, didn't need to run away to sea to see the world. The world came to see her instead – all spruced up for the camera in its holiday best.

I could see myself in shot after shot as if I were the presenter, not Debbie. Even Dad noticed how fed up I was.

'Look, Harry,' he said. 'We've got to make the best of it, you know. Let's go upstairs and mess about on my computer. I bet it's as good as Debbie Dream's any day.'

He was still being big brotherish, you see.

Next day, all the other kids were full of it. Just about everyone in my class, it seemed to me, had a mum or dad who was fixing up a Debbie Dream Holiday.

That's when they noticed how quiet
I was.

Dear Harry,

I'm delighted you've decided to accept my invitation to join the *Dream Holidays* team. As you know, we've been looking for a Trip Tester for some time, but we just couldn't find the right person.

Well, now we have! Please phone me as soon as possible so we can arrange a meeting to discuss the huge salary we'll pay you - as well as full expenses when you go on a trip, of course.

Shall I send my private helicopter to fetch you when you come to London?

Love from

Debbie Dream

Debbie Dream

Presenter and Chief Executive

You can imagine what they said to that.

All except Sareeka, that is.

Thank you, Sareeka.

Now she'd really dropped me in it.
The letter had been Dad's idea –
he'd helped me write it on his
computer because he'd felt so sorry
for me. But when it came to
postcards and holiday-snaps and a
video or two, I knew I'd be on my
own. He wasn't that much of a big
brother.

Still, at least I had time on my side.
Summer was such a long way off
maybe everyone would forget about
my Official Capacity before I had to
prove it was true.

Fat chance.

The rest of the winter was awful –
so awful it made everyone think of
their holidays.

'What's so wrong with the weather right now?' Roger asked. 'It's perfect for skiing.'

Then they all said:

Spring was even worse. Everyone longed for their holidays even more.

‘What’s so wrong with the weather right now?’ Mandy asked.

It’s perfect for scuba-diving!

Then they all said:

‘LOOKING FORWARD TO THE TRIP-TESTING, HARRY?’

Worst of all, though, was the summer. Would everyone be blown away before their holidays even arrived?

'What's so wrong with the weather right now?' Bernard asked.

It's perfect for fun-fairing!

Then they all said:

'LOOKING FORWARD TO THE TRIP-TESTING, HARRY?'

By now I'd got the message. Well, I'm not stupid, am I?

For some reason, don't ask me why, none of them believed in my Official Capacity! I was really, truly glad when school eventually broke up and they all went off on the same day to do their stupid loafing, skiing, scuba-diving, fun-fairing, highland gaming and safari-ing.

By the time I got home from school, I felt really sorry for myself.

Now I was stuck with Granpa while everyone else was having fun.

And in a few weeks time they'd all be back saying, 'HOW WAS THE TRIP-TESTING, HARRY?'

I was so fed up I needed a holiday.

Six holidays, actually. With postcards and happy-snaps and maybe a video or two to show what a good time I'd had.

Just a moment.

For someone like me – someone with a bit of Official Capacity about him – how hard could it be to fake a few of those holidays? After all, we'd got all the equipment I needed here at home. And I still had some money left over from my birthday.

Plus your talent, Harry.

How could I have forgotten my talent?

I didn't have to travel very far, either. On the edge of town, only a car ride away, we had *Leisure Land* – a complex which included a sports centre, an aquarium, a pool, a zoo and an amusement park.

So I set off at once with Granpa tagging along too. His job, according to Mum, was to "keep an eye on me" and make sure I stayed out of trouble.

I ask you. Nobody trusts anybody
these days.

To my surprise, though, our visits
were MEGA-BADLY-GOOD!

Partly this was because I got lucky right from the start. While Granpa and I were queuing up for tickets I got talking to a lady called Cass.

She laughed a lot when I explained what I was up to.

Actually, this turned out to be very useful because Granpa was a complete no-no when it came to doing tricky things with Dad's video gear. Pretty soon Cass and I let him doze off in the sun while we got on with it.

Of course, I had to be highly
organised . . .

HOLIDAY Spot	LOCATION	STUFF NEEDED	LEADING TO...
Loafing about (Sharon)	POOL	pencil and paper	postcard (back)
Swinging about (Bernard)	Amusement Park	Video	movie
Heave-hoing (Sareeka)	Sports Centre	Camera and Laptop	Newspaper page
Swooshing about (Roger)	Dry-ski slope	Video	Sports report
Glugging about (Mandy)	Aquarium	Camera and Laptop	Glossy magazine
Monkeying about (Tracey)	ZOO	Camera	Postcard (front)

STAR: HARRY WRITER: HARRY
DIRECTOR: HARRY NON-EXECUTIVE DIRECTOR: Granpa
EVERYTHING ELSE: CASS

We discovered a problem straightaway. Since it was my holiday I had to be in every scene . . . so how could I be the writer and director as well?

It wasn't easy I can tell you. Cass was lucky to be working with someone as talented as me. She was lucky I was so generous, too. I let her play with all Dad's video equipment as much as she liked. Also I let her sort out any snags that cropped up with the staff at *Leisure Land*. She was quite good at that.

39

40

41

I had a clear idea of how my videos, postcards and happy-snaps would look.

THE DAILY GOSSIP

TUESDAY

HARRY McHARRY
THE HIGHLAND CHAMPION!
Report by Finlay MacTrebble

Caber-tossing, throwing the hammer, sword-dancing and playing the bagpipes all come easily to Harry McHarry, Holiday Hero of the Highlands. He won everything! Afterwards, presented with a gold cup in the shape of a Haggis, Harry said he owed everything to TV presenter, Debbie Dream.

VIEWcam

SPORTS SPECIAL

What amazed me was how long it all took.

Even though I was absolutely ace,

and Cass was pretty good too,

a whole fortnight had gone by
before we had finished. By then,
Granpa had become
Snoozing Champion
of the Universe and
Cass and I were the
best of mates.

'Harry,' she said on our last day at
Leisure Land, 'you will take good
care of all this wonderful stuff,
won't you?'

Seriously cool, see?

Actually, as I tucked her card in my pocket, I knew I'd miss Cass quite a lot as well. One day, when I was older, I might even make her my girlfriend.

After that the real work began.
As soon as I'd got all the material
together . . .

. . . I began
to cut . . .

. . . stick . . .

. . . and colour . . .

. . . and tap things out on the
computer. Mum and Dad were
astonished.

Studious? I wasn't even sure what
that word meant.

By the time the holidays were over I was ready to face Sharon, Bernard, Sareeka, Roger, Mandy and Tracey again. I was pretty sure I was back in control. Or I was till they showed me what they'd brought back with them.

It was dazzling.

I'd never seen such postcards and
videos and happy snaps.
It made my stuff look . . .
well, homemade.
Had working with
Cass held me
back a bit,
I wondered?

Then, when they'd finished showing
off to each other, they all turned to
me. I knew what they were going to
say:

HOW WAS THE TRIP-TESTING, HARRY?

I wanted to die, honestly.

Instead, I went all tight-lipped.
'Great,' I said. 'Really great.'

'Let's see what you've got, then,'
said Sareeka, as sweet as ever.

'All of it,' I nodded. 'But it's top-secret. No one's allowed to look at it until the next series of *Dream Holidays*. On Debbie's orders.'

Mandy and Tracey were too busy giggling to say anything.

It was awful.

I couldn't wait for the end of school. I mean, a kid can only stand so much, right? Especially when he knows it's going to go on and on and on . . .

Halfway home, I stopped on the bridge across the river. Should I throw the box in, I wondered?

I held it over the water.

It was touch and go, I admit.

But, somehow I just couldn't let go
– not when I remembered all the
fun it had given me.

When I pushed open our front door
I wished I'd got rid of me *as well as*
the box, though. Now it was Mum
and Dad giggling their heads off.

Harry, you sly old dog! You didn't tell us you were going to be a TV star!

'A girl from *Dream Holidays* has just phoned us,' Mum said. 'She says the special programme about holidays at home is going ahead – Debbie loves the idea. She wants to make sure you've kept all the material safe. What material, Harry?'

But already I was fumbling in my pocket. I pulled out Cass's card.

There was a message on the back.

Dear Harry,
I was afraid to tell you I work for Debbie Dream in case it put you off. Guard this material with your life, though! I'll be in touch.
Love Cass

And on the front it said:

DREAM PRODUCTIONS LTD
CASSANDRA YARDLEY

PRODUCER

Already I could see myself co-presenting the *Dream Holidays Special*. Mum and Dad would be in the audience, of course, plus Gran and Granpa, not to mention all my uncles and aunts and cousins, and not forgetting Mrs Cadett our head teacher and Miss Hobbs our class teacher and Mrs Frisby our welfare lady. Why, if they asked me nicely, I might even find seats for Sharon, Bernard, Sareeka, Roger, Mandy and Tracey.

There was no point in being mean, after all. Not when you're someone like me . . .